The Lost Fairy

Marian Broderick

Illustrated by Aileen Caffrey

THE O'BRIEN PRESS
DUBLIN

First published 2001 by The O'Brien Press Ltd,
20 Victoria Road, Dublin 6, Ireland.
Tel: +353 1 4923333; Fax: +353 1 4922777
E-mail: books@obrien.ie
Website: www.obrien.ie
Reprinted 2002.

ISBN: 0-86278-725-4

British Library Cataloguing-in-Publication Data
Broderick, Marian
The lost fairy. - (O'Brien flyers ; 9)
1.Fairies - Juvenile fiction 2.Christmas stories
3.Children's stories
I.Title II.Caffrey, Aileen
823.9'14[J]

1 2 3 4 5 6 7 8 9 10
02 03 04 05 06 07

The O'Brien Press receives
assistance from

arts
council
schomhairle
ealaíon

Editing, typesetting, layout, design: The O'Brien Press Ltd
Illustrations: Aileen Caffrey
Printing: Cox and Wyman Ltd

TO:

Joe, Róisín, Edel and Áine

with lots of love

Chapter 1

Perfect Flora

Flora the Fairy sat at the very top
of the Christmas tree and looked
down at the family.

There was Mummy, Daddy,
Terry the Teenager, Lily the Little
and Patch the Puppy.

They were a nice family as families go. A bit silly maybe, but happy and generous.

But Flora herself was **gorgeous** – and she knew it.

She had big brown eyes, a perfect nose and curly golden hair. She was **extremely pretty** and **extremely proud** of herself.

Flora was also extremely **old**. In fact, she was older than everyone in the family – even Mummy and Daddy. Of course, because she was a fairy, she looked just the same as when she was brand new.

She had sat on her very first tree when Lily the Little's great-grandma was a little girl herself. And that was ninety years ago!

Flora remembered it well:

the horses clip-clopping,

the sleigh-bells ringing,

the smell of chestnuts roasting.

Flora wore a tiny, sparkly crown and held a little wand with a glittery jewel. Lily's great-grandma had made these for her ninety years ago.

She wore white silk shoes, which Lily's grandma had made sixty years ago.

She wore a rose-pink dress, which Lily's mother had made thirty years ago.

Flora **LOVED** being a fairy.

You didn't have to do much (which was just as well because Flora was very lazy).

You always looked perfect (which Flora liked because she was very vain).

But, best of all, at Christmas time the fairy was the **most important** person in the whole house – or so they'd told Flora in Fairy School.

Much more important than those cheeky snowmen halfway down the tree.

And **miles** more important than those silly reindeer below them.

Flora smirked. They all had to look up to her, like it or not.

But Flora was nervous of one
creature on the tree: the bright star
two branches below her.

She had heard – and it was hard to
believe – that some families put a **star**
at the top of the tree instead of a fairy!!

Sometimes Flora could see the star looking longingly at the top of the tree ...

Whenever she caught him at it, she shook his branch so he fell further down.

After all, Flora thought smugly, **she** was the one who made Christmas happen, not that silly star.

Flora the Fairy was the reason
Santa called to the house every
Christmas.

The rules were:

FAIRY'S RULES

• Make up a
song about the list of presents
and who is getting what.
• Sing it at
the top of your voice from
the top of the tree, so
that Santa can hear.

If Flora wasn't sitting there, singing the list of presents at the stroke of midnight on Christmas Eve, no-one would get anything!

It would be a DISASTER!

Flora had been taught this at Fairy School, so she believed it was absolutely **true**.

(Of course, Santa came to houses where the **star** was on top of the tree, and even houses where there was no tree at all, but Flora didn't know that.)

By now, Flora had this year's song off by heart. She'd been a bit lazy and just changed the words of *Jingle Bells*.

Santa wouldn't mind. *Jingle Bells* was one of his favourites.

Flora's Song

Santa Claus, Santa Claus
Flying through the sky
Please come down our chimney
And drop those presents by

Oh! Santa Claus, Santa Claus
Dashing through the sky
Don't forget to call on us
And let those presents fly.

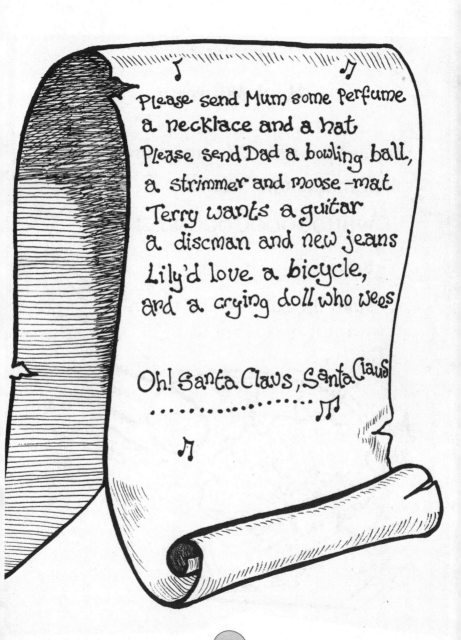

Chapter 2

Mad Mummy

It was Christmas Eve, and a breeze blew through the window.

WHHOOOOOOOOOOSSSSSHHHH!

Bang!

Flora the Fairy fell off the tree.

Flora lay on the floor. What, in the name of all that was sparkly, was she supposed to do now?

She couldn't move much. Fairies weren't meant to. They were meant to sit at the top of Christmas trees, looking perfect, and singing to Santa.

Occasionally a fairy might have trouble with an inquisitive fly or a pine needle in the wrong place.

But nobody in Fairy School had said anything about lying face-down with a mouthful of **carpet**.

Just then, Mummy came in.
She blew up balloons and she
hung up streamers.

'Help! Help!' squeaked Flora.
'Put me back on the tree!' But
Mummy didn't hear her.

She threw her wand at
Mummy. Nothing.

Mummy wrapped presents, tied bows, made phone calls. She was doing so many things at the same time, her arms looked like a windmill.

Finally, she spotted Flora and picked her up. 'How did you get there?' she asked in surprise. And she gave Flora a big, lipsticky kiss. 'Flora the Fairy belongs on the tree,' she said fondly.

'Gerroff!' said Flora crossly.
'You'll mess up my face. Just put
me back on the tree so I can do
my job!'

There was a thud from the
hall. 'The post,' Mummy
exclaimed. 'Oh great, *more* cards!'

And she tucked Flora under
her arm as she collected a huge
pile of envelopes from the
letter-box.

'No! NO!' Flora cried. 'Forget the cards! Take me back to the tree, the tree, the TREE!!'

But it was too late. Mummy dropped Flora on the desk and began to read the cards.

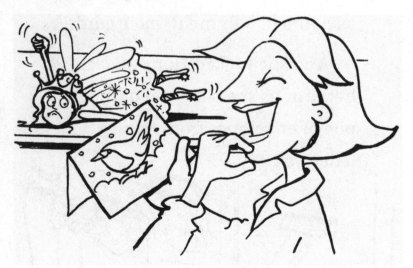

'One from Mrs Bird – robins in the snow; one from Aunty Jess ... '

And she forgot all about Flora.

Flora looked longingly at the shiny green tree, far away at the other end of the room.

Was it her imagination, or had the star **moved up** a branch?

Flora howled. 'Naughty Mummy!
Muddled, mixed-up, mad Mummy!
You won't be getting perfume,
jewellery or a hat! I'll ask Santa to
give you washing-up liquid, a
flea-collar and a bat!'

Chapter 3

Dopey Daddy

Daddy came in. He hung up
stockings, he blew up more
balloons and put up even more
streamers.

'Help!' said Flora, in a **really**
cross little voice. 'The tree! The
tree! I must get back to the tree!'

Daddy ignored her.

Flora took off her tiny, sparkly crown and threw it at him. Nothing.

Daddy put logs on the fire, fixed some broken fairy-lights, hung mistletoe over the door and put holly on all the pictures. He was doing so many things at the same time, his arms looked like an aeroplane propellor.

Then at last, **at long last**, he spotted Flora.

'Well, well!' said Daddy. 'I suppose I'd better pop this creature back on the tree.'

'About time,' grumbled ungrateful Flora.

But then something caught Daddy's eye.

It was a picture of a nice, fat, brown turkey in the cookery book on the desk.

'Oops!' said Daddy. 'I nearly forgot. It's my turn to make the stuffing this year. I'll use Grandma's recipe.'

'No, No, NO!' screamed Flora.

But it was too late. Daddy put the cookery book under one arm and Flora under the other.

When he got to the kitchen he dropped Flora in the sink and began to chop onions and herbs and make breadcrumbs.

And he forgot all about poor Flora.

'Bad Daddy!' spluttered Flora angrily, her mouth **full** of smelly onion skins.

She gazed anxiously at the shadow of the tree, far, far away in the other room.

She thought she could see the outline of the star. Was she imagining things or had he moved up **even higher**?

Flora screeched. 'Daft, dippy, dopey Daddy! You won't be getting a bowling ball, a strimmer or mouse-mat this Christmas!

I'll fix it so you get toilet rolls, rusty scissors and a ... a ... cowpat! Ha!'

Chapter 4

Terrible Terry

It was getting late on Christmas Eve.
Terry the Teenager came into the
kitchen. He looked in the fridge and
opened the cupboards. He checked the
biscuit box and picked a bit of icing
off the cake.

'Help! Help!' squealed Flora from
the sink. 'Take me back to the
tree! Now! PRONTO!' Flora took
off one of her silk shoes and
threw it at Terry.

By now her dress was torn and
her eyes were dirty-black instead
of velvet brown. She was a **MESS!**

Terry ate crisps, mince pies,
nuts and chocolates. He drank
coke, orange and lemonade. He
ate and drank so many things at
the same time his mouth looked
like a cement mixer.

But at last, at long last, he spotted
Flora and picked her up. 'I suppose
that **stupid** fairy should go back on
the pathetic tree,' laughed Terry the
Teenager. 'Boy, is she ugly!'

'Stupid?!' fumed Flora, 'Pathetic?!
Ugly?!'

But then something caught
Terry's eye.

It was a big stack of CDs.

'Oh, *cool*!' said Terry, 'these
must be for me!'

'No, stop – they're rubbish!' yelled
Flora.

But it was too late. Terry grabbed
the CDs and ate and drank all the
way upstairs.

He threw Flora the Fairy
straight into the laundry basket
and began to play the music.

And he forgot all about poor
Flora.

'Terrible teenager!' howled Flora, through a mouthful of dirty socks. 'Tubby, twerpy, teenaged twit!

I'll fix you! You won't be getting a guitar, a Discman or new jeans.

Instead you'll be getting a wheelbarrow, a toothbrush and ... green beans!'

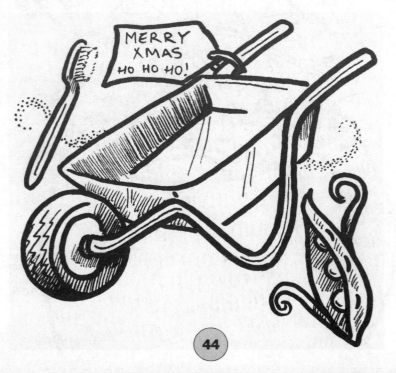

Poor Flora. She was further
away from the tree than ever
now.

Who knew what was
happening downstairs?

Chapter 5

Pesky Patch

It was late on Christmas Eve. Soon it would be getting dark.

Patch the Puppy came into Terry's bedroom. He chewed trainers and tore comics; he sniffed at socks and snuffled at the dirty sweaters in the laundry basket.

This time Flora didn't shout for help. She didn't even squeak. Instead she tried to keep very, very quiet.

'Oh no,' she whimpered to herself, 'not the **dog**!'

'Woof, woof-woof-woof!' barked Patch, 'Woof-woof ... '

And Patch the Puppy grabbed
Flora the Fairy in his teeth. He chewed
and growled all the way downstairs,
and Flora's head hit every step.

'The t ... t ... tree?' whispered Flora
hopefully, between thumps.

But something outside in the yard had caught Patch's eye.

It was his food bowl – and it was **FULL**.

'Woof!' barked Patch happily, in a way that sounded a bit like 'Yum-yum!'

He dropped Flora beside his bowl and began to slurp his food. He dribbled and slavered and gulped, until Flora was **completely** covered in dog slobber.

'Yeuch! Beastly beast!' wailed Flora, her mouth full of dog hair.

'You poopy, pongy, pesky pup! What on earth am I going to do NOW?'

Patch burped, picked Flora up again and buried her in the mud, like a bone. Only her head was sticking out.

'Woof!' he barked cheekily as he ran away.

Chapter 6

Lily the Little

Flora was further away from the tree than ever – she wasn't even in the house! But she could just see it through the window, green and welcoming. Home.

And the star was only a **teensy**, tiny little bit away from the top of the tree!

Flora the Fairy burst into tears.

Just then, Lily the Little came out.

Lily did not rush and fuss or chop and dust, or eat and drink or chew and tear.

She lined up her dolls and made them dance.

She pretended she was a queen, she pretended she was a soldier.

She hopped on one foot, and she told a joke to Patch.

And then finally, **at long last**, Lily saw Flora the Fairy, up to her neck in the mud.

Flora had a very, **very** dirty
face (with traces of lipstick on it),
very, very tangled hair (with bits
of parsley in it), and doggy
teeth-marks (with slobber in
them) on her soft skin.

She was no longer very pretty
and no longer very proud.

'Help!' cried the poor fairy humbly. '**Please**, please help!'

It was the first time Flora had **ever** said 'please' in her life.

Lily gazed at Flora. 'OK,' she said.

Flora the Fairy's dirty-black eyes opened wide under her tangled yellow and green hair.

'You can hear me!' she breathed.

'Of course I can!' laughed Lily. 'Everyone younger than eight-and-a-half can hear fairies. Didn't they teach you that in Fairy School?'

And Lily gently picked Flora up.

Lily took Flora inside and washed the fairy's face until it was clean and pink and her eyes were velvety brown again.

She brushed and combed Flora's hair until it gleamed like gold and the curls bounced.

Then Lily got out the sewing basket. She made Flora a **beautiful** rose-pink dress – just like her mother had done thirty years before.

She sewed Flora a pair of silk shoes – just like her grandma had done sixty years before.

And she made Flora a crown out of silver paper and a wand out of a matchstick – just like her great-grandma had done ninety years before.

Finally, Lily got her favourite fluorescent-pink plastic brooch and pinned it on Flora's new dress. It was her own special touch.

'Now!' she said. 'You're Flora the **Fluorescent** Fairy.'

Lily carried Flora over to the Christmas tree. She took down a silver ornament and held it up to Flora.

Flora gazed at herself in the silver ball. Once again, she was perfect, pretty, and very, very proud.

But this time Flora wasn't just proud of herself – this time she was proud of Lily.

'Lily the Little,' she proclaimed, waving her brand new wand. 'From now on you will be known as Lily the Lion-hearted, Lily the Loyal, and Lily the Lovely. Thank you, Lily!'

'You're very welcome,' said Lily.

Flora looked at the tree. The star was now almost in **her** place.

'Not for long!' she thought. Still, she had to admit that he did shine rather nicely – he wasn't as sparkly as she was, of course, but not bad ...

'Lily,' said Flora. 'When you put me back on the tree can you put my friend, the Star, beside me?'

And Lily placed the Star on the top of the tree.

Flora the Fluorescent Fairy sat
beside him, right at the very top of the
tree – where they both belonged.